THE CLASSIC TALES OF

Brer Rabbit

ILLUSTRATED BY
DON DAILY

FROM STORIES COLLECTED BY
JOEL CHANDLER HARRIS

COURAGE
BOOKS

AN IMPRINT OF RUNNING PRESS
PHILADELPHIA • LONDON

Introduction

Welcome to the Old Plantation, a place where rabbits and foxes and turtles play tricks on one another, and all of them somehow get caught up in the joyous laughter and music of life.

These are the tales of the crafty Brer Rabbit, Brer Fox, and their friends, playful folktales that have their roots in traditional African tales. These are stories full of character, history, and humor.

Told and retold for hundreds of years, the folktales were collected in 1880 by American newspaperman Joel Chandler Harris, who published them in *Uncle Remus: His Songs and Sayings*. Harris created the character named Uncle Remus, a grandfatherly storyteller who had once been a slave. In a rich, southern dialect, Uncle Remus related the adventures of Brer Rabbit and his friends to a little boy from the "Big House" on the Old Plantation.

The seven tales in this young reader's version were retold from Harris's original book of stories. The language in this retelling has been modernized, but care has been taken to retain the humor, the music, and the truth of these wonderful stories. For these stories aren't just about rabbits and foxes. These are stories about all of us.

To my family, Renee, Joey, and Susie
—Don Daily

Contents

Brer Fox, Brer Rabbit, Brer Bear, and the Peanut Patch

rer Fox had the best peanut patch in the country. It was full of lush, green vines bursting with plump peanuts that were just about to ripen. All the other creatures on the Old Plantation were mighty envious of Brer Fox— except for Brer Rabbit.

Brer Rabbit would have been
envious, too, if he hadn't found a way to
take advantage of the situation. Brer Rabbit
decided to wait until the peanuts were ripe, and then sneak
through a hole in the fence to snatch whatever peanuts he could.

Sure enough, just as soon as the peanuts were ripe, Brer Fox got up
bright and early to check on his patch. Right away he discovered that
someone had been stealing peanuts right off the vine!

Brer Fox was furious at the robber for ruining all his hard work, and
he was determined to catch the thief. Walking around the outskirts of

the patch, he found a hole in the fence—a hole
just the right size for a crafty rabbit to slip through. Right there,
Brer Fox set a trap. He bent down the branch of an old hickory tree
that stood beside the fence, and tied a rope to the end of it. At the
other end of the rope he tied a loop, and he set that loop down in
front of the hole in the fence, and weighed it down with a rock. Then
he covered it with leaves and grass.

Whoever stepped into that trap would be caught in the loop and
strung up in the hickory tree by the leg. Brer Fox was
pleased with himself. Now he could catch the thief.

That night, when Brer Rabbit sneaked through the
hole for more peanuts, he stepped right into the trap.
When he kicked away the rock, the loop flew up around
his leg, dragging him up into the air between heaven
and earth. He was mighty surprised to find himself
swinging upside-down from the hickory tree.

I hope I don't fall, thought Brer Rabbit, swinging back and forth. Then he had another thought: *I hope I do fall—otherwise, I might not get down*. And there he hung, swinging back and forth and thinking, trying to figure out what to tell Brer Fox to get out of this one.

Just as the sun began to rise, Brer Rabbit heard someone lumbering up the road behind him. By and by, Brer Bear ambled on up to the tree and saw Brer Rabbit hanging there, upside-down.

"Howdy, Brer Rabbit," said Brer Bear, tilting his head to look Brer Rabbit in the face. "How are you doing this fine morning?"

Brer Rabbit smiled a big smile. "Very fine, Brer Bear, very fine. No sir, you won't catch me complaining today!"

Brer Bear was puzzled—but it wasn't hard to puzzle Brer Bear. "What are you doing hanging up there in the elements, Brer Rabbit?" he asked.

"Well, truth be told, Brer Bear, I'm making a dollar a minute," said Brer Rabbit.

"A dollar a minute! How?"

"Brer Fox is paying me to keep watch over his peanut patch," Brer Rabbit explained. "Some thief has been stealing his goobers. Yessir, this is just about the best job I've ever had. Hanging upside-down gives you a whole new perspective on the world." Brer Rabbit paused. "You wouldn't—? Nah."

"Wouldn't what?" Brer Bear asked.

"Well, you wouldn't want to take over, would you? I mean, I know you've got family to feed, and you'd make a mighty fine watchbear. And a dollar a minute is nothing to sneeze at."

Brer Bear didn't much like the idea of hanging upside-down, but he liked the idea of making a dollar a minute. It wasn't long before Brer Bear let Brer Rabbit down, stuck his own leg through the loop, and took Brer Rabbit's place hanging upside-down from the tree. The branch hung so low that Brer Bear almost bumped his head on the ground as he dangled in the air.

"Enjoy yourself, Brer Bear," said Brer Rabbit. Then he ran to Brer Fox's house.

"Oh Brer Fox! Brer Fox! Wake up and I'll show you who's been stealing your peanuts," Brer Rabbit called from outside Brer Fox's window. Right away, Brer Fox got up and ran off to the patch with Brer Rabbit.

There they saw Brer Bear, hanging upside-down from the tree and grinning bigger than a hyena.

"Howdy, Brer Fox!" said Brer Bear. "I'm glad I could be—OWW!" Brer Bear didn't finish—Brer Fox had thwacked him in the behind.

"What'd you do that for? I'm only help—OUCH!" Brer Bear stopped again as Brer Fox swung his stick once more.

It went on like this for about half an hour. Every time Brer Bear tried to explain, Brer Fox thwacked him again. And every time Brer Fox thwacked him, Brer Bear tried even harder to explain.

While all this was going on, Brer Rabbit slipped away and hid in a nearby pond. He knew that once the thwacking was over, Brer Bear would be coming after him. So he stayed in the pond until he heard Brer Bear furiously lumbering up the road.

Only Brer Rabbit's eyes poked out above the mud. Brer Bear thought he was a bullfrog.

"Howdy, Brer Bullfrog," grumbled Brer Bear. "You seen Brer Rabbit go by?"

"He just went by—CHUGARUMP!" said Brer Rabbit. "He went that away—CHUGARUMP!" pointing his eyes to the east.

"Mighty obliged, Brer Bullfrog," said Brer Bear. And off he lumbered.

Brer Rabbit stayed in the pond until Brer Bear was well out of sight. Then he headed off the other way for home, laughing all the way.

Brer Rabbit Goes Fishing for Suckers

Everyone on the Old Plantation felt sorry for Brer Fox. He had worked so hard all spring on his peanut patch, clearing, and planting, and sowing, only to have his harvest stolen. So all the creatures gathered together to help Brer Fox plant a new patch of peanuts.

Brer Bear, Brer Raccoon, and even Brer Rabbit showed up to help Brer Fox replant. Brer Rabbit was feeling guilty because he was the one who had stolen all the peanuts, so he helped, too.

They got busy clearing the peanut patch, pulling up the old vines and making rows to plant new ones. Now, the weather was mighty hot, and soon Brer Rabbit, who wasn't much of a worker in the first place, got tired.

Brer Rabbit didn't want the others to know that he was tired. He knew full well that he was a lazy creature, but he hated for others to know. So he needed a plan.

"Is anyone hot?" asked Brer Rabbit, wiping the sweat from his nose.

"I sure am," said Brer Bear.

"Me, too," said Brer Fox.

"Me three," added Brer Raccoon.

"Well then, suppose I go get us some water," said Brer Rabbit, running off into the nearby woods before anyone could say otherwise.

The woods were
nice and shady, and
Brer Rabbit felt much
better being out of the
heat. As he looked
about, he saw an old stone
well, with two buckets
hanging from the top.

Brer Rabbit was supposed
to be fetching water, but that
wasn't his first thought. His first thought
was how nice and cool it would be to take a little bath.

So into one of the buckets he hopped, and down he went. At first,
the water was nice and cool. But then it got really cool, and soon after

that it turned quite cold. Brer Rabbit started to shiver, and decided it was time to go up.

There was only one problem—he had no way to raise himself to the top. He had left the other bucket on the ground at the top of the well! Brer Rabbit started to get scared. There he was, alone and cold, in the bottom of a well, far away from everyone else.

As a matter of fact, he wasn't that far away from everyone. Brer Fox never let Brer Rabbit go too far out of sight. He knew that Brer Rabbit was always plotting something. So he had followed Brer Rabbit.

From behind a nearby tree, Brer Fox had seen Brer Rabbit hop into the bucket. *Now why is he going down there?* Brer Fox thought to himself. *There's nothing down there but cold water. And Brer Rabbit's much too smart to get himself stuck down there for no good reason. He must be keeping something in the old well—something he doesn't want us to see.*

Brer Fox thought he had it all figured out. The old well must be where Brer Rabbit kept his treasures! What treasures, Brer Fox didn't know. But he decided right then and there to make a deal with Brer Rabbit.

"Breeerrrrr Rabbittttt"— his voice echoed down the well to the shivering rabbit. "What are you doing down there?"

Brer Rabbit knew that Brer Fox was his only chance to get out. He thought quickly and answered, "I'm fishing for suckers."

"Are there many of them down there?" asked Brer Fox.

"Scores and scores," said Brer Rabbit. "Come on down and see."

Brer Fox knew that there weren't any suckers down there, but he did want to see Brer Rabbit's treasure. So he hopped into the second bucket, and down he went. As he rode down, Brer Rabbit started riding up in the other bucket.

Halfway down, going pretty fast, Brer Fox passed Brer Rabbit, who was singing this song:

"Good-bye, Brer Fox, take care of your clothes
For this is the way the world goes.
Some go up and some go down,
But you'll get to the bottom safe and sound."

Brer Fox just waved good-bye in confusion. When he reached the bottom, he began looking around for the treasure. Sometime later, Brer Rabbit sent the others to help him out.

And ever since then, whenever Brer Rabbit wanted a good laugh, he'd ask Brer Fox if he'd like to go fishing for suckers.

Dead Foxes
Tell No Tales

It was a bright summer day in the country. Birds were chirping, squirrels were bounding about, and the sun was smiling down on all the world. It seemed as if all the animals were smiling back—all the animals, that is, except for Brer Fox.

Brer Fox was strolling down the road, looking mighty downhearted, and kicking a pebble. When it stopped, he'd amble on up to it and kick it again.

In this way he slowly made his way down the road, ignoring everything around him—which was why he nearly ran over Brer Wolf. Brer Wolf was resting by the side of the road, looking longingly at the sheep in a nearby pasture.

"Watch where you're going, Brer Fox," said Brer Wolf. "Why, you nearly ran me down! Now I've got to start my counting all over again!"

Brer Fox just looked up at him, and didn't even apologize. Then he looked back down, kicked the pebble, and moved on.

Brer Wolf could tell that something wasn't right. So he decided to follow Brer Fox down the road, and see what was what.

"What's got you stewing?" he asked Brer Fox.

"Guess," said Brer Fox.

"Are you hungry?"

"Nope."

"Are you tired?"

"Nope."

"Are you angry?"

"Now you're getting somewhere," said Brer Fox, kicking up a cloud of dust and missing the pebble entirely.

"At who?" asked Brer Wolf.

"I'll give you a hint," said Brer Fox, finally giving Brer Wolf his full attention. "He's fast, and he's furry, and he's got long brown ears, and he's a big pain in my neck!" Brer Wolf knew immediately—he could only be complaining about Brer Rabbit.

"What did he do to make you look stupid this time?" Brer Wolf asked.

"This time, nothing," said Brer Fox. "I'm just sick and tired of his shenanigans. He's always one up on me. I've got to find a way to get back at him."

"Well, I'd be happy to help, Brer Fox."

The plan was simple—they would somehow lure Brer Rabbit to Brer Fox's house, and show him a thing or two with a large club when he arrived.

"But how are we gonna get him to come?" asked Brer Fox, "I mean, he's so suspicious of me that he'd only consider coming inside if he knew I was lying down dead."

Brer Wolf scratched his head. "Then you will be dead," said Brer Wolf.

Now Brer Fox scratched his head. "Correct me if I'm wrong, Brer Wolf, but if I'm dead, it's going to be awfully difficult for me to show *anything* to Brer Rabbit, let alone a thing or two."

"You won't actually be dead," Brer Wolf explained. "That's just what we'll tell Brer Rabbit. You'll be lying down pretending, and he'll come running in to see if it's true—and then you'll nab him!"

This made sense to Brer Fox—if there was anything he understood well, it was nabbing.

So Brer Fox went back to his house, to lie down and practice being "dead" for a while before Brer Rabbit came. And Brer Wolf went knocking on Brer Rabbit's door.

KNOCK! KNOCK! KNOCK!

"Who's there?" said Brer Rabbit from inside his house.

"Brer Wolf," said Brer Wolf, "with some awful bad news."

"If it's that you're standing outside my house, I can already see that," said Brer Rabbit, looking out the little window.

"Something even worse," said Brer Wolf, missing the joke completely. "Brer Fox is dead."

Brer Rabbit opened the door.

"Dead?" said Brer Rabbit. "How did it happen?"

"I'm not really sure," said Brer Wolf. "I just saw him lying there in his bed, and when I tried to shake him awake, he kept on lying there."

"You wouldn't be pulling my leg, would you?" said Brer Rabbit.

"No, Wolf's Honor," said Brer Wolf, raising his right paw. Now, Wolf's Honor didn't mean much to Brer Rabbit, but it was enough to get him interested in going over to Brer Fox's house to see what was going on.

He and Brer Wolf quickly made their way over to Brer Fox's house. Peeking in through the window, Brer Rabbit couldn't believe his eyes! There he saw Brer Fox lying on the bed, looking as dead as can be. But *looking* dead wasn't the same as *being* dead, and Brer Rabbit knew this. So he decided to test Brer Fox.

"Brer Fox, are you sleeping?" he called. No answer.

"Brer Fox, you lazy excuse for a forest animal, get up!" he called again. Still no answer.

Brer Rabbit was beginning to doubt his doubting.

But he had to be sure before he went inside. He turned to Brer Wolf. "Well, Brer Fox sure looks like he's dead. But he doesn't really act dead."

"What do you mean, he doesn't act dead?" asked Brer Wolf. "He's lying there stone cold, isn't he?"

"Sure," said Brer Rabbit, "but everyone knows that dead people lift up their legs and holler, '*Yahoo!*' when a visitor comes by."

"Oh! Why—why that's true!" said Brer Wolf, not wanting to look dumb.

Well, Brer Fox may have been dead, but he didn't want to look dumb either. So he immediately lifted his legs, and at the top of his lungs, yelled,

"YAAAHHHOOOOOOOO!"

Then he waited for Brer Rabbit to enter.

"I'm glad to see you're feeling better, Brer Fox," said Brer Rabbit. And he tore off fast for home, before Brer Fox and Brer Wolf could say another word.

The Great Race

O f all the creatures on the Old Plantation, one of the smallest—and one of the smartest—was Brer Turtle.

Now, Brer Turtle was a calm, quiet creature who always considered things very seriously. When he spoke, he spoke slowly, choosing his words carefully.

So it seemed all the more surprising when Brer Turtle got himself into a race against Brer Rabbit.

It all started one day near the pond. Brer Turtle was just waking up and beginning to emerge from his shell when he noticed something strange in front of him—a very large pink nose and whiskers, just outside his shell.

"Heellooooo innnn theeerrre," echoed the nose and whiskers.

Brer Turtle thought he was dreaming.

"I said, Hellooooooooo," repeated the nose. Then it laughed.

This was no dream. Brer Turtle slowly stuck out his neck to see what was what.

There sat Brer Rabbit, sitting comfortably on a stone and chewing on a reed. Brer Turtle should have known.

"Morning, Brer Turtle," said Brer Rabbit. "I don't mind saying that you're one of the slowest wakers I've ever met."

Brer Turtle yawned. "I may be a slow waker, Brer Rabbit, but I'm faster than you'll ever be—once I get myself going and have my morning fish." He meant brain-wise, of course.

But Brer Rabbit didn't know what the turtle meant. He didn't realize that Brer Turtle was talking about fast thinking—so he took his statement as a challenge.

"So, you think you're faster than me, huh?"

"Yup," said Brer Turtle. "Always have been, always will be." He was quite proud of his mind.

"Then I guess you wouldn't mind joining me in a little test, eh?" said Brer Rabbit.

"Not a bit," said Brer Turtle. He liked a good quiz. "What'll it be—reading, writing or 'rithmatic?"

Brer Rabbit laughed. "You'll need more than that to beat me, Brer Turtle." He got up, and threw down his reed at the turtle's feet. "High noon. My house. Once around the Old Plantation. Be there."

Brer Turtle realized that he had misunderstood Brer Rabbit's challenge. *Once around the Old Plantation? What kind of test is that? He knows he's faster than I am! But I can't let Brer Rabbit get one up on me,* Brer Turtle thought. *I've got to find a way to beat him.*

Brer Rabbit was far and away the fastest animal on the Old Plantation. Brer Turtle knew that there was no way he could fairly beat him. But then again, there was nothing fair about Brer Rabbit—so why play fair?

After he had his morning fish, Brer Turtle was thinking much more clearly. He had three sons, each one the spitting image of his father. Now Brer Turtle had a plan.

Soon it was high noon. Brer Turtle sent each of his sons to hide in a different spot along the path of the race. Then he met Brer Rabbit at the starting line.

"Ready to lose, Brer Rabbit?" asked Brer Turtle.

"The day I lose to you is the day I dance on my ears," sniffed Brer Rabbit.

Brer Buzzard was the judge. "All right you two. Once around the Old Plantation. On your marks. . ." Brer Rabbit and Brer Turtle took their marks.

"Get set. . ."

Brer Rabbit and Brer Turtle set their feet.

"GO!"

And off they went.

Brer Rabbit sped out of sight. Brer Turtle scurried along as fast as he could—for about five feet. Then he began to walk slowly down the path. When Brer Turtle had rounded the bend and the starting line was out of sight, he doubled back through the woods to wait near the finish line.

Brer Rabbit knew he was way ahead of Brer Turtle, so when he rounded a curve where a huge oak tree stood, he decided to take a little rest. Brer Rabbit leaned against the shady trunk and closed his eyes.

"Mighty nice here in the shade, isn't it?" said a familiar voice. Brer Rabbit opened his eyes—there was Brer Turtle! Actually, it was Brer Turtle's eldest son, but Brer Rabbit thought it was Brer Turtle.

"How—What! Wh—Where? You!" said Brer Rabbit.

"Well said," said Brer Turtle's son.

Brer Rabbit was too confused to speak. He got up and took off running even faster than before.

But just when he rounded another bend he tripped, and fell, ears over heels. Brer Rabbit got up and walked back to see what he'd tripped over. From a distance, it looked like a rock.

But as he got closer, he saw that it was no rock. He had tripped over a shell—Brer Turtle's shell, to be exact.

Brer Turtle (actually, it was Brer Turtle's second son) poked his head out. "Have a nice trip?" he asked.

"But I! You! Back there!" said Brer Rabbit.

"Couldn't have said it any better," said Brer Turtle's second son.

"Hmmmph!" said Brer Rabbit, speeding off again.

Brer Rabbit was taking no more chances. No rests, no rocks—just a straight line to the finish.

For a while it was smooth running, and Brer Rabbit was flying down the road at full speed. He felt sure that the race was his—that is, until he rounded the next bend and spotted a small creature ahead.

Brer Rabbit squinted to see what it was—it couldn't possibly be— no! Nevertheless, he turned on the speed, and in a few moments, he was neck and neck with Brer Turtle again!

Brer Turtle's third son smiled at the rabbit, and kept moving.

"No! This! How?" said Brer Rabbit, his eyes wide.

"I'd love to chat," said Brer Turtle's third son, "but I'm in the middle of a race right now.

Gotta go."

Brer Rabbit was stunned. He picked up speed, passed the turtle quickly, and headed towards the finish line.

Brer Rabbit rounded the final bend. The finish line was just ahead! Brer Rabbit looked back to see that Brer Turtle had dropped out of sight. Brer Rabbit dug in his heels, and headed for home.

He was running faster than he had ever run. He was running so fast that when he did cross the finish line moments later, he had to grab a nearby tree to stop himself from running past the spectators.

"Hah!" he yelled, panting heavily but dancing with victory, "I've won, I've won!"

"What did you win?" asked a slow voice.

"The race, you fool, I won the ra—"

Brer Rabbit stopped cold. There, right in front of him, was Brer Turtle.

"I don't know what race you won," said Brer Turtle, "but it wasn't this one."

Brer Rabbit couldn't believe his eyes. Brer Turtle just looked at him and said, "Well, go ahead."

"Go ahead what?" asked Brer Rabbit.

"Go ahead and dance on your ears," said Brer Turtle, calling over his three sons. Each one was carrying a musical instrument.

Brer Turtle laughed loud and slow. "I can't wait to see this," he said.

Brer Rabbit couldn't speak. He had been beaten, in more ways than one. He couldn't deny it. So he stood on his head, began moving his ears, and danced to the music of the turtles.

Why Mr. Possum Loves Peace

ne day Brer Possum was feeling bored and lonely, so he dropped by to visit Brer Raccoon. The two friends decided it was time for their monthly race. They raced every month, just for a little fun and exercise.

In the middle of the race, they heard Mr. Dog coming. They tried to figure out what to do, but the figuring came too late, and Mr. Dog attacked.

Brer Possum keeled over and played dead, leaving Brer Raccoon to fight Mr. Dog. Brer Raccoon was small, but he still managed to scratch Mr. Dog pretty well. Mr. Dog scampered off as soon as he could, and so did Brer Raccoon.

When the coast was clear, Brer Possum slowly opened his eyes and ran away, too.

Later that day, Brer Raccoon's path crossed with Brer Possum. Brer Raccoon was angry with his friend and he accused him of being a coward.

"I am not!" cried Brer Possum. "I knew you'd beat Mr. Dog just like I would have! Why, I was no more afraid of him than I am of you."

"Then why did you keel over like you were dead?" said Brer Raccoon. "Seems to me it was because you were scared of fighting."

Brer Possum just laughed. "Not scared of fighting," said Brer Possum, holding his belly to keep it from jiggling too much, "Scared of tickling. I'm probably the most ticklish animal you'll ever meet," said Brer Possum, "and I knew I'd be tickled to death if I got in a scrape with Mr. Dog."

Brer Raccoon laughed at the thought and forgave Brer Possum.

And to this day, Brer Possum will keel over and play dead if you try to tickle him.

Brer Fox Goes Hunting

One day, Brer Fox decided he needed to get his mind off his encounters with Brer Rabbit. So he decided to distract himself by going hunting.

Brer Fox left for the woods early in the morning, hours before the sun peeked up over the hills. He spent most of the day in the woods, and it was a good day of hunting—he bagged a whole mess of game. The last thing on his mind was Brer Rabbit.

On the way home, he sang to himself as he ambled down the road. At least, he thought he was singing to himself. But as it happened, someone heard Brer Fox's singing as he passed by the old oak tree about a mile from his house.

And that someone was Brer Rabbit. He was catching a little
bunny nap around the back of the old oak. Right then he heard Brer
Fox's song:

> "I've got a mess of game, and it sure is sweet
>
> It took a bit of work, but I'm glad to have the meat
>
> I'm gonna go home and cook it right up
>
> I'm just about as happy as a newborn pup!"

Brer Rabbit liked the thought that Brer Fox had so much game.

Brer Rabbit got up and ran through the woods ahead of Brer Fox.

Brer Fox was out of sight just around the bend,

so Brer Rabbit lay down in the middle of the

road, silent as a log.

Brer Fox rounded the bend, and stopped his singing immediately. There in the middle of the road was the fattest rabbit he'd ever seen.

"My goodness, if that isn't the fattest rabbit I've ever seen! Why, that rabbit would feed me for two or three months." Brer Rabbit didn't really appreciate being called fat, but he kept still. Brer Fox looked at the bag of game in his other hand.

"Still, I've got plenty of game already," Brer Fox told himself. "I guess I'll go home first, and come back for the rabbit later." He started humming and left the rabbit behind.

Brer Rabbit was not about to give up. So he ran through the woods again, up ahead of Brer Fox, and lay back down in the road.

Brer Fox nearly dropped his bag when he rounded the bend. There was another dead rabbit! And this one looked even fatter than the

first! (Brer Rabbit had puffed out his stomach and cheeks to look a little larger.) He also noticed an abandoned wheelbarrow nearby.

"Well, I'll be an uncle's monkey—a moncle's unkey—a—whatever. Another rabbit! I can't pass this up twice." Right then and there, he decided that it was worth his while to leave his game, go back for the first rabbit, bring it up around the bend, and then take both rabbits and the game home in the wheelbarrow.

So he dropped his game and, singing to himself, he went back after the first rabbit.

When he was out of sight, Brer Rabbit unpuffed his cheeks, got up, took the bag full of Brer Fox's game, and set out for home.

He ate very well that week. Several days later, he met Brer Fox on the road.

"I heard you went hunting the other day," Brer Rabbit chuckled to Brer Fox. "What did you catch?"

"I caught a bagful of sense a little too late," grumbled Brer Fox.

Brer Fox, Brer Rabbit, and the Tar-Baby

t was the hottest day of the year on the Old Plantation. It was so hot that the potatoes underground were nearly cooking in their skins. Brer Fox sat at home, trying to cool himself off with a willow branch. He sat there waving the branch at his face, desperately working to get a breeze going.

But he was working up more of a sweat than a breeze, so there he sat sweating, and waving, and thinking.

It was the thinking that finally got Brer Fox upset. He was trying to remember the cooler days in his life, the days when he was relaxed, and calm, and well, cool. He thought that if he could remember those days, it might help to cool him off now.

Trouble was, he couldn't remember a day like that recently. In fact, he couldn't even remember such a day in the past six months. He's always been upset and irritable, and there was only one reason why: Brer Rabbit. Brer Fox couldn't remember a relaxing day since Brer Rabbit had been around.

Well, maybe it was the heat, and maybe it was the thinking, but Brer Fox decided then and there that he had had enough. He decided that it was his turn to show Brer Rabbit who he was dealing with.

Brer Fox threw aside the willow branch and went out to his shed. He took out a bucket of tar and a can of turpentine, and mixed them together. What he got was a large black glob, stickier than honey and smellier than a dozen skunks.

Then he took the glob in the bucket, grabbed an old straw hat, a white comb, and a couple of white buttons, and walked the mile to the main road.

When he got to the main road, Brer Fox dumped the glob out onto a large log right in the center of the road. He put the hat on top of the glob, shoved the two buttons in for eyes, stuck the comb in for a grinning mouth, and his masterpiece was ready. The Tar-Baby was born.

Brer Fox smiled a sneaky smile and laughed low. Then he went into the bushes nearby, and waited for Brer Rabbit. He knew that Brer Rabbit would come along eventually—it was hot, and Brer Rabbit would have to pass this way to get to the well.

By and by, Brer Rabbit came down the road, walking and skipping lippity-clippity, lippity-clippity toward the well. *He's just as sassy as a jaybird,* Brer Fox thought to himself. *I can't wait until he gets his.* Brer Rabbit made his way happily down the road—until he saw Tar-Baby sitting on the log.

Now, Brer Rabbit was crafty, but he was also a friendly creature, always greeting everyone who passed his way—especially strangers. And he didn't recognize the figure in front of him.

Brer Rabbit walked up and stuck out his hand. "Good morning, stranger! Is it hot enough for you?" Brer Rabbit said in his friendliest greeting voice.

The Tar-Baby just sat there smiling, and didn't say a word. Brer Fox kept lying low in the bushes.

Brer Rabbit tried again. "I said good morning! How are you doing?" Brer Fox squinted his eyes to see better, and lay low, and the Tar-Baby didn't say a word.

Brer Rabbit was getting overheated. "What's the matter—you deaf?" he shouted. The Tar-Baby smiled, silent and still, and Brer Fox lay low.

"You're mighty stuck up, that's what the matter is," said Brer Rabbit, his furry face turning red with anger. "And I'm going to unstick you unless you answer me real soon, if you get my meaning!"

Brer Fox swallowed his laughter, and the Tar-Baby didn't make a sound.

"That's it!" spat Brer Rabbit. "I'm going to have to teach you a lesson. If you don't take off your hat to say 'Howdy' I'm going to bust you right open!" Well, needless to say, the Tar-Baby didn't speak, and he didn't remove his hat.

Brer Rabbit figured he had put up with enough. He had greeted this stranger like a friend, and had been treated like an enemy. Brer Rabbit drew back his fist, and with all his might, he swung straight for the Tar-Baby's head.

Well, his fist went right into the Tar-Baby—and got stuck.

Brer Rabbit pulled back, but the Tar-Baby wouldn't let go. "If you don't let me loose," said Brer Rabbit, "I'll knock you again!" The Tar-Baby didn't let loose, and Brer Rabbit drew back his other hand, and swung again. Now both hands were stuck, and the Tar-Baby still didn't say a word, and Brer Fox kept on lying low.

Brer Rabbit pulled and tugged, but he couldn't get away. "Turn me loose before I kick the stuffing out of you!" he said. The Tar-Baby didn't answer, so Brer Rabbit kicked him with his right foot—which got stuck. He kicked again with his left foot—stuck again.

As if he hadn't had enough, Brer Rabbit yelled that if the Tar-Baby didn't let him loose he'd butt him right in the head. The Tar-Baby didn't, and Brer Rabbit butted, and now his forehead was stuck, too.

Brer Fox was done lying low. He got up from the bushes and sauntered out, just as innocent as a newborn pup.

"Howdy, Brer Rabbit," said Brer Fox. "You look sort of stuck up this morning." Then Brer Fox burst into laughter and rolled on the ground, laughing until he couldn't laugh anymore.

Brer Rabbit just sat there, stuck, and the Tar-Baby sat there grinning, and didn't say a word.

By the time Brer Fox stopped laughing, a full hour had passed. Brer Rabbit didn't say anything throughout the whole laughing episode—he didn't want to give Brer Fox the pleasure of hearing him complain.

By and by, Brer Fox began to realize that this was more than a good practical joke he'd pulled. This was the opportunity of a lifetime, a moment that could not go to waste. This was Brer Fox's chance to get rid of Brer Rabbit once and for all.

Brer Fox sat on a stump by the side of the road, stroking his chin and thinking out loud. Brer Rabbit just sat there stuck—there wasn't much else he could do.

"Well, I suspect I've got you this time, Brer Rabbit," Brer Fox finally said.

Brer Rabbit would have looked a little bit frightened if he could have, but his face was stuck on the Tar-Baby, so he couldn't move.

Brer Fox kept on speaking. "You've been acting like the boss of the whole plantation for too long now. Well, I think it's finally time the boss was replaced." Brer Fox let out a chuckle. "The best thing of all is that you got yourself where you are now—nobody asked you to get stuck. But you're always sticking your ears into somebody else's business. Now you're stuck for good."

With that, Brer Fox got up, and brushed off his fur.

"Now don't you go anywhere until I get back. I'm going to search for some kindling, and when I get back, I'm going to have myself a little rabbit barbecue."

Brer Rabbit had to think fast. He shifted his eyes to the left, looking for a way out. Nothing over there. He shifted his eyes to the right—and there he saw his answer. There, not twenty yards away, was a prickly briar patch. It was just the kind of briar patch that would get the tar off his fur, if he could only get himself into it.

Brer Rabbit knew he had to get into that patch—it was his only chance. But he would have to trick Brer Fox. Then Brer Rabbit had an idea.

"I don't care what you do with me, Brer Fox, as long as you don't fling me into that briar patch over there," Brer Rabbit pleaded.

Brer Fox didn't answer right away. He was having a hard time finding any sticks for kindling.

"Well, it looks like you lucked out, Brer Rabbit," said Brer Fox eventually, coming out of the brush. "I can't find any kindling to make a fire. So I guess I'll have to hang you." He began digging in his pocket for rope.

"Hang me as high as you please, Brer Fox," said Brer Rabbit, "but just don't fling me into the briar patch." Now he sounded a bit weepy.

Brer Fox dug deep into his pockets and came up empty. "Well, I'm out of rope," said Brer Fox, "so I guess I'll have to drown you." Brer Fox began looking around for a nearby river or pond.

"Drown me if you must, sink me as deep as you want, Brer Fox," said Brer Rabbit, "but please, PLEASE don't throw me into the briar patch!"

Now Brer Fox could find no water. He was getting a bit frustrated. "I can't see any water around here," said Brer Fox.

This was Brer Rabbit's chance. "Do whatever you like, Brer Fox," said Brer Rabbit. "Leave me here to starve. Thrash me good. Tickle me to death, even. But please, if you have any kindness in your cold fox's heart, please don't throw me into the briar patch!"

Brer Fox took the bait like a hungry trout.

"Ah-HA! So, you don't want me to throw you into the briar patch, eh? Well, I'm afraid I'm out of time and you're out of luck—the briar patch it is!"

So Brer Fox picked up Brer Rabbit and the Tar-Baby and flung them both head over heels, ears over feet, into the briar patch—just like Brer Rabbit wanted.

When Brer Rabbit struck the bushes, a huge cloud of dust and briars flew up into the air. The briars prickled Brer Rabbit quite a bit, but they stuck themselves to Tar-Baby, and soon Brer Rabbit became completely unstuck from the Tar-Baby!

Meanwhile, Brer Fox stood looking over the briar patch, trying to see what had happened to Brer Rabbit.

Finally, the dust settled. Brer Fox looked closer. To his surprise, all that was left in the briar patch was the Tar-Baby, completely covered in briars.

"I told you not to throw me in there," called a voice. Brer Fox turned quickly to see Brer Rabbit calling to him.

"Maybe next time you'll listen," Brer Rabbit said. And with that, Brer Rabbit headed for home to clean the rest of the tar out of his fur, hippity-hopping, lippity-clippity, all the way home.

Cover and interior illustrations by Don Daily
Cover design by Frances J. Soo Ping Chow
Interior design by Nancy Loggins Gonzalez
Retold by David Borgenicht
Typography: Goudy Oldstyle

This book may be ordered by mail from the publisher.
But try your bookstore first!

Published by Courage Books, an imprint of
Running Press Book Publishers
125 South Twenty-second Street
Philadelphia, Pennsylvania 19103-4399

Visit us on the web!
www.runningpress.com